Rain

D0994617

In memory of my dad Lyuba with whom
I enjoyed watching thunderstorms.
M.S.

First published in the United Kingdom in 2000 by
David Bennett Books Limited, London House,
Great Eastern Wharf, Parkgate Road, London SW11 4NQ.

This paperback edition first published in 2001.

Text and illustrations copyright © 1999 Manya Stojic.
Manya Stojic asserts her moral right to be
identified as the author and illustrator of this work.

All rights reserved. No part of this publication
may be reproduced, stored in a retrieval system,
or transmitted by any means, electronic, mechanical,
photocopying or otherwise, without the prior
permission of the publisher.

BRITISH LIBRARY CATALOGUING-IN-PUBLICATION DATA:
A catalogue record for this book is available
from the British Library.

ISBN 1 85602 413 X
Printed In Hong Kong

Rain

WRITTEN AND ILLUSTRATED BY
MANYA STOJIC

DAVID BENNETT BOOKS

FALKIRK COUNCIL
LIBRARY SUPPORT
FOR SCHOOLS

It was hot.
Everything was hot and dry.

The red soil was hot and dry and cracked.

A porcupine sniffed around.
"It's time," she whispered.
"The rain is coming! I can smell it. I must tell the zebras."

Lightning **flashed.**
" **The rain is coming!** "
said the zebras.

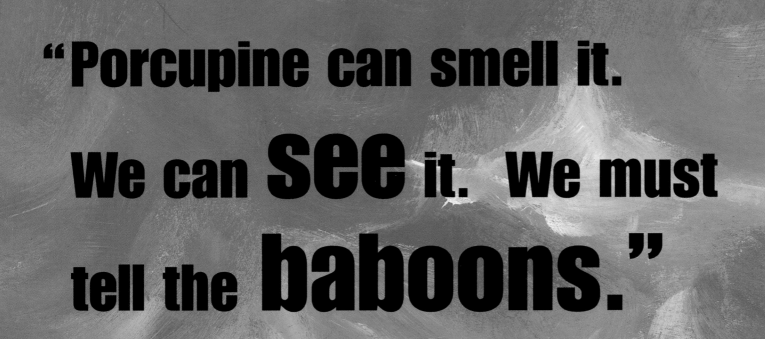

"Porcupine can smell it. We can **see** it. We must tell the **baboons**."

Thunder boomed.

"**The rain is coming!**"
cried the baboons.

"Porcupine
can smell it.
The zebras
can see it.

We can **hear** it.
We must tell
the **rhino.**"

A raindrop **splashed.**

"The rain is here!"
said the rhino.

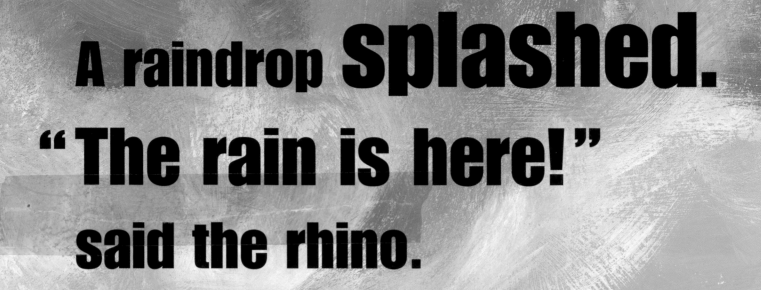

"Porcupine smelled it.
The zebras saw it.
The baboons heard it.

And I **felt** it.
I must tell
the **lion."**

The lion
spoke
in a
deep
purr.

"Yes, the rain is here.

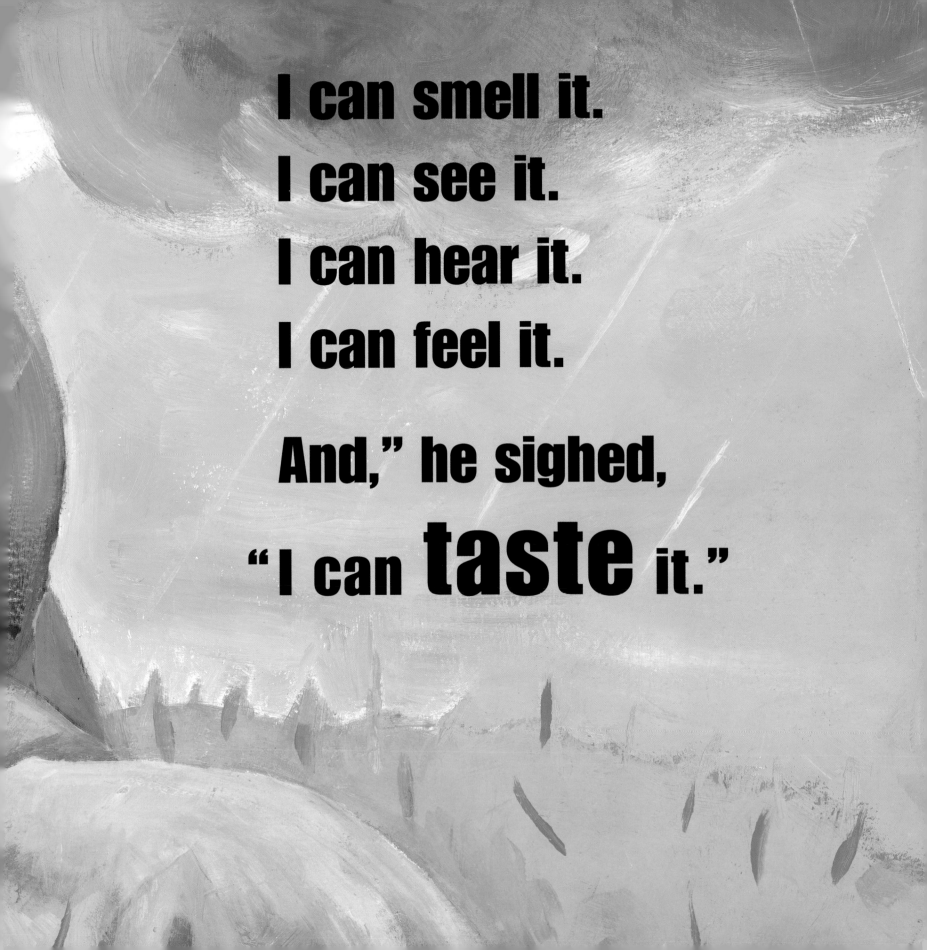

I can smell it.

I can see it.

I can hear it.

I can feel it.

And," he sighed,

"I can **taste** it."

It rained

and it

rained

and it

rained.

It rained until every river
gushed and **gurgled.**

It rained until every water hole
was **full.**

Then the rain stopped and everywhere long, feathery grasses grew from the soil.

Every tree began to sprout fresh, green leaves.

"I can't taste the rain now," purred the lion,

"but I can enjoy the shade of these **big, green leaves.**"

"I can't feel the rain now," said the rhino,

"but I can lie in the **cool, soft, squelchy mud.**"

"We can't hear the rain now," shouted the baboons,

"but we can eat

**fresh,
juicy fruit
from the trees."**

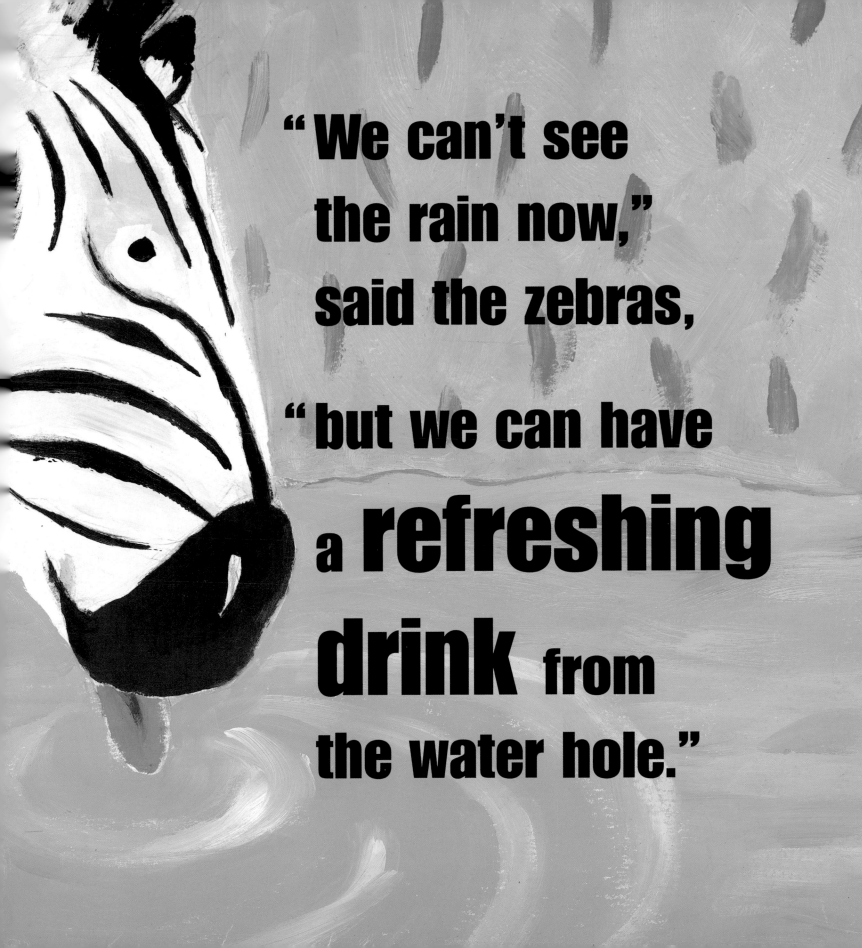

"We can't see the rain now," said the zebras, "but we can have a **refreshing drink** from the water hole."

"I can't smell the rain now," whispered the porcupine, "but **I know** that it will come back again. When it's **time.**"

The sun shone over the plain.

It was **hot.** Everything was drying out.

The red soil was hot and dry.

A tiny crack appeared.

FALKIRK COUNCIL
LIBRARY SUPPORT
FOR SCHOOLS